# THE CHRONICLES
# OF SPENCER DREW

## ADVENTURE ON
## MONKEY ISLAND

# THE CHRONICLES OF SPENCER DREW

# ADVENTURE ON MONKEY ISLAND

Robert Guy Spencer
and Becky Hall

The Book Guild Ltd
Sussex, England

First published in Great Britain in 2005 by
The Book Guild Ltd
25 High Street
Lewes, East Sussex
BN7 2LU

Typesetting in Palatino by
Keyboard Services, Luton, Bedfordshire

Printed in Great Britain by
CPI Bath

A catalogue record for this book is available from
The British Library

ISBN 1 85776 935 X

*This book is dedicated to Laura, Fliss and Tim.*

*Love Mummy*

*xxx*

# Contents

# Chapter 1

# *How it all Began*

Have I told you the story of how I lost my left eye? How Q replaced it with a tiger's eye? How it's no ordinary eye, but contains a small photocell that absorbs energy from daylight? How in the gloom of night you'll be amazed to see the explosion of light which blasts from my tiger's eye?

After my accident, where I lost my eye, I slipped into a coma and when I awoke found I had amazing powers of recollection and reasoning. Cool! And Mum was told that when I was unconscious I had some weird activity in areas of the human brain that are normally dormant, which even the doctors couldn't explain.

Have I told you any of these things? Well I have now! I don't think I'll tell you about the nightmares or the other things I can't quite explain ... I want to keep those things to myself.

It's the first week of my summer holiday with my real dad, Ronald Drew. I am Spencer Drew. I'm ten years old, nearly eleven.

Mum and Jimmy (that's my stepdad), now live in London. I live with them too. We have a big house, that's called a Victorian terrace, with a big barbecue in the courtyard. My bedroom is on the first floor.

Bliss, my big sister, is at drama college and stays here at the weekends. Her hair is always bright red like her bedroom, which she was allowed to paint because she's almost a grown-up. I'm going to paint my bedroom yellow when I'm older and dye my hair yellow or purple or both, as long as I don't leave any mess in the bathroom. Or Mum will go ballistic.

Mum and Dad split up when I was five years old. But Mum and Jimmy moved to London following my horrific accident, when I lost my left eye!

I don't remember too much about it and it didn't hurt because I was knocked out, well I mean I was unconscious, so sometimes people make it out to be worse than it actually was. I spent nearly three months in Great Ormond Street Hospital after the accident, so Jimmy and Mum bought a house in London to be closer to me.

I have a great doctor who I call 'Q' like in James Bond. His real name is Mr James Quinn, but Jimmy and I like to call him Q.

Losing my eye meant I had to wear a big bandage for ages, but for the past two weeks I have now got the coolest glass eye in the history of glass eyes!

Dr Quinn, I mean Q, knew I was really unhappy with the eye they were going to give me, so he asked me what sort of eye I would really like. Now ordinarily, I suppose, it would be one that matched the real one, but when I tried it out I even scared myself! I preferred seeing the patch on my face.

Mum was a bit cross because I wouldn't keep the lovely brown eye, but Q understood. He said I didn't have to wear a bandage any more, but he would be open to suggestions!

On the way home from the hospital I asked Mum to stop at the joke shop. That's where I got my first pirate's patch. Mum got all tearful again and said I looked so handsome with my dark curly hair flopping over my patch.

I think I've got crazy hair. It's not like Dad's or Mum's, although now it's longer the curls are getting straighter. It must be in the DNA. My Dad, Uncle Steven and cousin Ben have all got bright orange curly hair, whilst my other cousin, Toby, has completely white hair. How weird is that? By the way, underneath this week's colour my sister, Bliss, has got brown hair, like Mum's.

That night when I went to bed I had a fantastic dream. I was chasing someone in Poole Park in the night! And I had extraordinary strength and speed. I could even climb trees and see in the dark. The person I was chasing had done something bad, I don't know what, but I had to catch him. I felt so powerful and it was only just before I woke up that I saw who I was. I looked across the boating lake in Poole Park and to my disbelief, my reflection was not that of Spencer Drew but instead I was a tiger! A beautiful big tiger! Then

I heard Mum's voice telling me to 'Wakey, wakey, rise and shine, hang your knickers on the line!'

Mum says that every morning. Sometimes I think she treats me like I'm just a kid! *Hello Mum, I'm nearly eleven now!* Well, she had to whisper it to me in hospital, so as not to wake up the other children on the ward. She even whispered it in my ear when I was unconscious for three weeks. Mum says that's what woke me up.

Anyway, after that dream Mum let me phone Q. I said I wanted the eye of a tiger, but could it double as a torch too, so it would be more useful than just sitting there. Of course I didn't tell Mum I'd asked Q for the eye of a tiger or for it to double as a torch. I thought she might be cross, thinking I was cheeky, especially after refusing the lovely brown one, but hey, if you don't ask you don't get! That's my motto.

Mum did ask me what I had chosen. I bought myself some time and told her my new eye was a little *brighter* than my old eye. Well, that half-truth kept her off my back until our hospital appointment.

I won't say too much, but what I have learnt is that it must be a man thing! Q, Jimmy, Dad and of course me, think it's the coolest eye ever. But Mum isn't convinced!

I eased the situation in the consulting room by announcing that a gecko eye was my second choice. Given that information, Mum decided she preferred the tiger's eye after all! Of course geckos have got freaky bobble eyes that swivel about – now how daft do they think I am?

4

Bliss, my big sister, says I would look really handsome with a gecko eye, but I think she's being *ironic*!

I still wear my black pirate's patch and now I'm allowed to get my eye wet, which is good news for my holiday with Dad.

I couldn't wait for night-time so I could test out the built-in torch. As I've said, it doesn't need any batteries. It has a small photocell that absorbs energy from daylight. The only trouble is, there's no on or off switch. Wearing the pirate's patch preserves the power and sitting with my eye open in daylight will recharge it for nearly two hours torchlight. But I mustn't look into the sun or anything stupid like that. Of course I've been testing it loads. *And in the dark of my room I take the patch off and watch the laser light blast from my tiger's eye!*

I have had a home tutor, to catch up on my school work for the past three months. But something surprising has happened since my accident. Yes, you'll remember what I told you, I seem to be a lot smarter.

OK, pay attention. When I was unconscious, which I have no recollection of, I had lots of tests on my brain. Mum was told by Q that I had some weird activity in areas of the human brain that are normally dormant. They don't know if that is normal for me or a result of my accident, but since I woke up I am like the biggest big-head of useless information. I started reading waiting room magazines and remembering whole articles, then having opinions on things like animal spirits and Glastonbury 2004 and just about everything in the world! I think I started to freak Mum out. Bliss uses me to help finish her course work, on nineteenth-century poets; Jimmy just enjoys the conversations we have about James Bond, The Beatles, Nick Hornby, Homer Simpson and Kylie Minogue. Dad says I was always that clever.

It's a pity I didn't wake up like Spider Man instead of boring Brainy Memory Man! Still I should get straight A's in all my exams unless I lose my powers.

Q sent me all over the place for tests and it turns out I have what they call a photographic memory!

I'm annoyed I can remember so many other things, but I can't recall anything much about my horrific accident. After the initial impact of the car on my bicycle (when I lost my eye).

I haven't told you yet about the accident have I? Well, Dad and I were out enjoying ourselves in Poole Park on a normal Sunday afternoon, when a tall youth with spiky hair crashed into the man just a few feet in front of us. He knocked him down quite hard with his bicycle. I thought it was just an accident, but he grabbed a package from inside the man's jacket and sped off. Dad went to help the man and call the police on his mobile but I chased after the youth on my bike. Dad called to me to come back but I didn't listen. I thought I knew better!

And I did nearly catch up with him. I saw him leaning into a car handing over the package to someone. I was really close to the car and then suddenly it reversed back at high speed. I saw it coming back but I had no time to get away. All I remember was a cold hard thud and suddenly a burning pain through my eye. I'm sure you can guess what had happened.

I can recall trying to focus on the dark shadowy figure standing over me and then staring at the loose gravel next to my head, resting my gaze on a small *shiny black stone*. I don't know why, but it seemed terribly important that I reached out to grab the stone, tightening my grip on it as I fell into blackness.

A second later (well of course three weeks had elapsed in real time), I woke up with a hosepipe stuck down my throat and a straw stuck up my nose and needles stuck everywhere. You should have seen the amount of machinery with buttons and digital read-outs all around me.

But when I did wake up the first thing I actually saw was my mum with her head on the side of my bed, asleep, with a book open. Mum cried and cried for such a long time when I woke up, but I felt OK, well a whole lot better when they took out the plumbing.

I do remember the first words that my sobbing Mum said to me when I woke up. 'Oh, Spencer, your curly hair has grown so much since you've been asleep. You look so beautiful.'

The funny thing was, I didn't even notice I'd even

lost my left eye until Mum told me. I still had a bandage covering it so I couldn't see it was missing.

You know the rest; except that Dad has been staying with me at Mum and Jimmy's house on some weekends. And now, at last, I am fit enough to go and stay with Dad in my old home in Poole, Dorset. I really miss my Dad. He misses me too.

I'm really excited today, because Mum and Jimmy are driving me to Dad's house in Poole. That's the house I grew up in.

Dad says if the weather forecast is good we will go on a real adventure with my cousins Ben and Toby, and Uncle Steven. Uncle Steven is Dad's younger brother. He's fifty this year. I hope our adventure includes plenty of sailing!

I told my new friends in Great Ormond Street that I was going to have an adventure on my boat. Yeah, you should have seen their faces when I told them that. They didn't believe me when I told them I could sail Dad's boat. Even Mrs Epson, my new tutor, looked confused when I tried to tell her about *Splash* my dingy.

Mum is calling me down for breakfast. I'm already dressed. That will surprise her! Dad already has my wetsuit, oilskins and life-jacket. He says he's got me a new pair of trunks and a pair of bigger dingy boots. Good, because I seem to grow an inch every day at the moment!

Bliss is here with one of her girlfriends from college, she is called Pink! Just like that pop singer! I don't think Pink is her real name, but she is very pretty even with all those pins in her eyebrows and nose.

Bliss and Pink are house-sitting. Mum gave Bliss a long list of things to remember and I definitely heard Mum say *no parties...*

'Hey Spence, got something for you.'

Bliss puts out her hand, offering me a package wrapped with pink ribbon.

'Cool, thanks!'

Mmm, a pair of sunglasses, really hip ones that go round at the side and look like mirrors.

'Thanks, Bliss.'

'It will make a change from that awful pirate's patch!'

'No, I'll still wear that underneath!'

Bliss stares at me. 'Whatever Spence!'

Good, we're leaving. Shades on.

Bliss and Pink look very happy. I bet they want to watch Jimmy's satellite television all weekend. I like the cartoon channels, the same as Jimmy. Mum doesn't like television – well, sometimes she watches the music channel. I don't understand why anyone couldn't like television. When I'm retired I think I'll watch cartoons and James Bond films all day. I think if Mum watched more television she'd be as clever as Jimmy and me! In fact I think I'll tell her that...

Well, I did tell her, and she and Jimmy haven't stopped laughing yet.

Jimmy's got a really cool car now. It's the top of the range BMW, just like James Bond in *Tomorrow*

*Never Dies*. I pretend to be driving it by using my remote control handset, although it's really Mum's old broken mobile phone she gave me to play with. She's got a really fab one, but I'm *not* allowed to touch it. Well not since I got it wet. I was sure it was waterproof but Jimmy went bonkers when he found me testing it for buoyancy. Apparently it isn't waterproof like Mum's watch!

I'll soon be at my dad's. I take my new shades off. I like them but I really do prefer my pirate's patch.

When we arrive at Dad's house he is mowing the grass in the front garden. I'm sure he wants me to help him. I open the car door and rush up to Dad and give him a big hug and kiss. I gently push him away from the mower to make room for the expert. That's me.

'No, Spencer!'

But I know he'll be too busy talking to Mum to stop me. Oh, it's not working. Maybe it's broken or the plug has come out. What's wrong with it?

Dad has taken my case inside and it looks like Jimmy has disconnected the power lead from the garage extension.

'Your dad said, "No". And this stepdad agrees with him!'

I try and explain that my dad lets me do this, but Jimmy doesn't believe me.

'Spencer, when your dad is here with you and he can watch what you're up to, please feel free to lick your fingers and stick them in the socket,

10

in the meantime, I'll just make sure you don't electrocute yourself, OK?'

'OK, but Dad likes me to cut the grass...'

'Look, *Zorro*, you've already lost one eye, let's try not to lose anything else OK?'

I can see Jimmy is not budging from the extension lead. Dad and Mum are at last back outside. Mum gives me a big hug and kiss and the usual, be good, help Dad routine and don't forget to irrigate your eye with saline solution before bedtime.

Jimmy walks towards the car and wishes me a lovely holiday with Dad.

Now this is delicate. I want to give Jimmy a hug and kiss too, but Dad is here and I don't want to make him feel sad. But I'm feeling sad if I don't kiss Jimmy, so last chance I run to the driver's door that Jimmy has just opened and pretend to whisper something in his ear. I kiss his cheek and call him 'Smelly Pants', so loudly that Dad can hear me being rude to him. Nicely done, Spencer.

'I'm going to use my remote control on your car, so it makes you drive all wonky, flaky!'

That makes Mum and Jimmy laugh.

I feel a bit sad as Mum and Jimmy drive away. I wish they could come on our adventure too, but as Dad reminded me, they are both going back to work next week.

Dad says we're having tea with Uncle Steven tonight. I can't wait to see my cousins, Ben and Toby.

11

*　*　*

Dad and I eventually finish mowing the lawn, and yes, I manage not to blow myself up, so pooh to you Jimmy!

After the summer holidays I am going to start fencing lessons and tennis too. Not because I'm a spoilt brat, but it's just that since I lost my eye I don't have binocular vision. This is how people with two normal eyes see. I can't judge distances with just one eye, so I'm going to start some activities which will help me overcome this disability. Otherwise I will find ball sports more difficult and long-term things like driving a car could be difficult, so I will overcome this. It's really just making other bits of my brain work at calculating the distance instantly. I understand all of this because Q explained it to me and I can recall everything he said.

I haven't shown anyone my tiger's eye. All my family know, but I have asked everyone to keep it a secret. I like my tiger's eye, but wearing the patch over it makes me look cool and I don't want people to think I'm a circus freak. I want to get used to the way things are for me first.

Dad sometimes calls me Captain Pugwash. I don't mind. I like being a pirate. Of course I forget I look different to other boys and girls because of the patch.

I have noticed people stare but mostly they think I'm off to a fancy dress party.

*　*　*

Dad says I have to wash my face and hands before I go to Uncle Steven's.

I race down the road on my bike with Dad somewhere behind. He's too slow to wait for, but he won't mind, Uncle Steven only lives down the end of the cul-de-sac.

Dad didn't want me to have another bike to start with, but eventually he gave in. It's a real beauty, but I can see Dad is worried when I'm on it. Mum said just let him use it, let him be like a normal boy and don't worry. But I know it troubles him.

I throw my bike down in their back garden and burst in through the back door and rush into the lounge...

*Spencer is here!* Pay respect!

But suddenly my coolness has gone as I'm hugged to death by my Nanny, Grandad, Auntie Sarah and Uncle Steven. Ben, my eldest cousin who is fifteen years old is busy trying to concentrate on the television. Ben is extremely tall for his age and already looks like a man not a boy. He even has to shave. I take after Ben because I am really tall, too. He's gentle and kind and used to be playful before ... *puberty* (that's what I hear the adults say).

'Hi, Spencer.'

Toby, my other cousin, is twelve, short and thin but very tough and good at all sports. He tries to sound less enthusiastic about me being here. It doesn't matter – he always tries to act cool until he wants me to play or use my bike or scooter, but I like playing with him so that's OK. He and I sort of like not always getting on.

Later that evening Toby and I play chess. Toby is a champion chess player at his school.

'What's it like only having one eye, Spence?'

'Well, I've got one normal human eye and then of course I've got my special hyper-biotechnical tiger's eye which gives me night vision far beyond any human sight. It's all in the thousands of tiny mirrors which reflect light, mimicking a true eye of a tiger. I'd rather have this eye than two human eyes any day.'

Toby chuckles to himself. 'Can I see it then, Spence? This *amazing* tiger's eye of yours?'

'Sorry, Toby, I'm still keeping it covered up to keep out germs.'

I feel a bit mean not showing Toby, but I'm not really used to seeing it myself yet. And I think sometimes Toby can be a bit cruel.

'Well, I don't believe that load of rubbish about a tiger's eye!'

'That's OK. It sounds a bit unbelievable even to me. *Checkmate.*'

Toby wasn't too happy that I beat him at chess. Especially as that *was* the first time I've ever beaten him at chess. Mind you I did read that book *How to Be a Champion Chess Player* in hospital.

'What's that necklace all about, Spencer? It looks a bit girlie to me.'

Toby has noticed my lucky black stone. The doctors and nurses found it in my hand when I was rushed into hospital. Apparently it took them ages for me to let go of it. They gave it to Dad to look after. Dad made it into a pendant with a silver square surrounding the black stone and a leather neck tie which if it breaks can easily be replaced. Dad and Mum call it my lucky stone.

'It's my lucky stone, Toby; it protects the person who wears it.'

'*Yeah right*... Can I have a go, then?'

I shake my head. But Toby can be very persistent.

'So, if I kick you in the crown jewels that stupid stone will protect you?'

'*No!*'

That made me jump. Dad practically leapt out of the armchair and became very animated and nearly scared my pants off, and Toby's, I think.

'Toby, it belongs to Spencer. It's not a toy and I don't want Spencer to lose it. If you find a lucky stone I'll make you a pendant too.'

'Oh ... OK, Uncle Ronnie...'

Dad was really quite forceful over that. Blimey, I didn't know he had it in him! I could see fear in his eyes and hear it in the tone of his voice too.

Toby and I played most of the evening together and only sometimes did he disappear round the block on my bike.

Ben came out a few times but rather like Bliss, kept himself to himself. I did offer him a go on my bike and scooter but he didn't want to. Sometimes he does, but not today. I think he will play more when I'm a teenager. I hope Ben wants to play a bit when we go on our big adventure.

The evening ended well; Dad and Uncle Steven planned our adventure and we all went home happily to sleep. I am so excited. Our adventure starts on Sunday!

Have I told you how happy I feel tonight?

## Chapter 2

# Monkey Island and Bloodcurdling Pirates

At last it's Sunday morning. Last night I dreamt I was a tiger again. It made me feel strange. This time in my dream I saw a snake – it was twisting itself around my arm, before raising its hissing face to my eye... I woke up with a jump that shook me. I don't know what it means. Dad says it's just a dream and it doesn't mean anything, but it feels very familiar to me; it disturbs me like a puzzle that needs to be solved.

Ben and Toby spent last night on our big cruiser called *Florence*. We moor *Florence* on 'C' pontoon at Poole Yacht Club. It will soon be time to set off on our adventure. Just like James Bond!

I still wish that Grandad could come with us – but he's very old and stiff and needs to go to the toilet a lot!

It has been decided that on this adventure we are taking three boats. Grandad's launch (without Grandad), *Dougal* (the rubber inflatable) and *Splash* (my Mirror sailing dingy).

* * *

Nanny, Grandad and Auntie Sarah have come to wave us off. Goodbye to everybody in the whole world! Uncle Steven is in Grandad's launch with most of the kit. Ben and Toby are sailing *Splash*, but she's not going very fast. She doesn't have an engine like *Dougal*, but she does have a set of oars. Toby is helming.

Dad and I are in *Dougal*. Uncle Steven has started to zigzag and is making lots of wash for us to go through. Dad and I are getting soaked!

'We'll get you for that, Uncle Steven!'

This is fantastic!

We have turned left out of Poole Yacht Club and cut across to Wills Cut which joins the Wych Channel. I know the names of the channels and buoys because Dad has been taking me round the harbour since I was four weeks old. I've also got an Admiralty chart of Poole Harbour up in my bedroom in London. Mum gave it to me. When I was a bit younger I used to pretend I was sailing *Splash* or Dad's cruiser, using my baseball bat as a tiller at the end of the bed.

A channel is like a road in the water. You have to stay between the red and green markers otherwise you'll find yourself stuck on the bottom. Even though I'm now a freaky brainbox I knew all these things before my accident. Mind you, it did pay off reading all Dad's *Practical Boat Owner* and *Yachting Monthly* magazines when I was in hospital. What I have learnt about satellite navigation and marine safety equipment is …

incredibly boring, but sadly memorable in my case!

The island we are going to camp on is called Monkey Island and it is very, very private. It is owned by a friend of Dad and Uncle Steven's. The owner is away on holiday at the moment but says we can pitch our tents on his island, which means we'll be the only people there.

I think our island is called Monkey Island because there's a big monkey tree, or was it a big monkey living in a tree? Anyway, I hope there really are monkeys living on Monkey Island because monkeys are friendly to humans.

Apart from those human-eating monkeys I read about last month in the *National Geographic*... Anyway, we were all monkeys a long, long time ago. Shall I tell you about Darwin's Theory of Evolution? Doh ... here I go again...

'Dad, are there any real monkeys living on Monkey Island?'

'Well, not at this precise moment, Spencer, but very shortly there are three very big noisy monkeys arriving!'

'Ha, ha, Dad, very funny. Tell me really.'

'I believe there were some monkeys inhabiting the island during Victorian times, they were owned originally by a rich merchant, who let them run wild on the island. However, according to history, they soon learnt to swim. They crossed over the harbour onto the mainland causing mischief and mayhem.'

'What happened to them? Are they still around?'

'No, no, I shouldn't think so. They were mostly

caught and put in captivity. They were wild monkeys and the merchant was forbidden to keep any more wild animals.'

'But there might still be one left on the island, maybe?'

'Well, very doubtful, Spencer. It would be a very, very old and pretty decrepit monkey if it were still alive today after 100 years.'

'But surely they were capable of reproduction?'

Dad stops and stares at me. 'Yes, I suppose, so Spencer... Where do you get these conversations from? Do you think you could try being ten instead of twenty?'

Anyway, this will be our very own secret island! Toby and I have already planned to look for buried treasure!

We gently putter round to the south side of Monkey Island. We are coming in really close to the shore now. Dad has slowed down to speak to Uncle Steven.

'That looks quite a safe place to come in. There's a small pier just over to the right the other side of those overhanging trees. Maybe it's deep enough for the launch, or if not we can keep *Splash* alongside the pier and anchor the launch.'

'I'll take a look. Stay close, and if I get stuck you can tow me off.'

Dad and I bring *Dougal* in. It's like a large horseshoe shape, the beach, and further up there are lots of big sand dunes with wild grasses growing out. To the right as we head into the shore is a large mass of land covered in huge overhanging trees jutting right out over the water. It looks like a great place to play hide and seek. I bet there are loads of fossils here too!

Dad carries the bottles of drinking water, the tents, Ben's fishing rods and tackle up the beach. We pull the rubber boat as far as we can, but Dad says Uncle Steven will help lift it further up later on. Dad secures the painter to a big rock.

We hurry across to the other side of the overhanging trees to where Ben and Toby are ferrying the gear ashore.

Ben and Toby are on their third trip to the launch, taking as much kit as they can manage. We're taking the kit to the beach just behind the pier. Ben and Toby are back alongside Grandad's launch again. Then, as Uncle Steven passes over a large kitbag to Toby, Ben gets up and rushes to look over the side of *Splash*.

'Wow! Look at the size of that fish! It's just gone under the stern of Grandad's launch! Look, everybody!'

The sudden extra weight of Ben over the same side as Toby sends the dingy and its crew badly out of control, losing all balance. Ben launches himself towards the rear of the dingy grabbing the tiller to prevent a head-first dive into the harbour as Toby manages to save himself by grabbing the side of *Splash*, but not before he lets go of the kitbag Uncle Steven has just passed him. *Splash!*

Now *that* was funny...

Luckily Uncle Steven looks like he has already caught something using his boat-hook, and up from the water comes the kitbag!

21

'Sorry about that, Toby,' says Ben.

'That's OK, Ben. Anyway, it's your kit that got wet!'

'I thought that was your bag!'

'Well, technically it is my bag, but you borrowed mine for the regatta because the zip was broken on yours and we never swapped them back!'

I really wish Jimmy could have seen this. Dad and I are laughing so much.

'Don't worry, Ben, we can dry your pants in the sunshine!' chuckles Uncle Steven.

'Yes, Ben, that will keep the seagulls away!' Dad shouts.

And everyone bursts out laughing again.

At last we are all unpacked. Ben's scary underpants are drying over *Dougal* in the afternoon sunshine and he has now gone off on his own to catch some fish.

Dad and Uncle Steven have started pitching their tent. Theirs is quite close to the beach, but well above the high tide mark.

Toby and I manage to get our tent up without too many arguments (and we only had to be pulled apart once by our dads).

Now to go exploring … Toby and I are going to hunt for fossils and buried treasure. I'm going to keep my good eye out for any of those doddery old monkeys. Dad and Uncle Steven say we can go, but we must stay together and be back at camp at three o'clock.

We set off into the sand dunes which eventually

lead into some dense bushes and trees. Toby finds a really good stick, which he uses to break through the jungle.

'Toby, can you help find me a stick like yours, please?'

'OK, Spence. Why don't we go over to that really big tree? There is bound to be one there.'

Toby and I set off towards the big tree. It's fantastic, one of its lower branches bends right down, nearly touching the ground, and you can climb right along and reach up to the next branch. We both shuffle along the branch and up to the next one and sit with our legs either side of it.

Sitting up here is brilliant. We just sit together not saying anything for ages.

We can see Ben lying down on his tummy on the wooden pier looking down into the water over the edge.

'I wonder what he's looking at.'

'Maybe he's seen some treasure?'

'Or a pair of his underpants being worn by a giant crab!'

Toby thinks that is really funny.

'Well if it was a dirty pair of Ben's underpants the crab would be dead by now!'

We head back to camp as it's nearly three o'clock. Uncle Steven is already beginning to prepare our barbecue supper. Ben, Toby and yours truly go for a swim!

Ben wants to rig a rope swing in one of the trees

overhanging the water. Dad says he can, but not too high. Ben fixes a rope over a big branch so we can swing and drop into the water. Dad tests it first to make sure the branch is strong enough to take our weight, and then we all take turns.

Letting go is a bit scary, but fun, and depending on how high you swing before you drop makes for a bigger splash! So far Ben makes the biggest splash, followed by a *tsunami* (which by the way is a giant tidal wave. And Jimmy said I was a boring old git for reading the *National Geographic* in hospital!) Anyway, throwing ourselves into the water makes for lots of shouting and laughter. This is heaven.

We play for ages whilst poor Uncle Steven is the galley slave. I can smell the sausages cooking which is making me feel really hungry.

'Supper is ready, you lubbers.'

I am starving. We don't even have to wash our hands before supper. It's still very warm in the sun. We just wrap towels round our tummies after drying our hands and faces. Uncle Steven serves up a fantastic barbecued supper, minus the king prawns for me!

'Dad, do you think I could borrow Grandad's binoculars?' I ask.

'Yes, as long as they go back into the launch if she's taken out. Remember, they are part of the ship's safety equipment.'

'Oh yes, I will, Dad, I promise. Can Toby and I get them tonight, so we can keep a lookout for pirates?'

'Well ... I'll take you round in *Dougal* after supper. I'd like to check her anchor hasn't dragged now the tide has turned.'

'Thanks, Dad.'

We eat until we nearly burst (and Toby and I end up spreadeagled on the sand about to explode).

'Hey, Spence, Toby, if you want to get Grandad's binoculars, give us a hand carrying *Dougal* down the beach.'

Toby and I groan as we lift ourselves up off the sand. Life-jackets back on and off we go. The tide is coming back in now. We leave the beach and head left, round the overhanging trees. The pier is only about twenty feet the other side of the trees.

We arrive at Grandad's launch. Dad and Toby hold her alongside whilst I jump on board and find Grandad's binoculars.

'Dad, can Toby and I sit on the end of the pier for a while?'

'Well, it's getting colder now the sun is going down, Spence. If you come back and put your fleeces on with your life-jackets on top, then the answer is yes. But *no* swimming after supper, you know the rules. Come back after sunset.'

'We will, Dad. Thanks.'

Toby and I return to the pier with our warm fleeces and life-jackets on. Playing hide and seek on the way, in the shadows of the hanging leaves and twisted tree trunks. Ben didn't want to come with us. He's listening to his Nirvana CD on his Walkman.

We dangle our legs over the end of the pier, watching the sun go down. All too quickly it disappears over the horizon. In just a few moments the sky seems completely black. The temperature drops, and I want to see my Dad.

'Shall we go back now?'

'Let's wait a few more minutes.'

'Are you scared of the dark Toby?'

'No.'

But I think he is. I am.

'It's really dark now. Maybe we should head back to our camp.'

Phew, I am *so* relieved to hear Toby say that!

We leave the wooden pier and head towards the overhanging trees.

'What's that noise, Toby?'

We can both hear a boat engine approaching from the left of the channel.

'I don't know. Maybe it's Uncle Ronnie or Dad in *Dougal* coming to look for us.'

'No, it's not the right sound for *Dougal*'s outboard. This sounds a much bigger engine. Maybe it's the man that lives on the island come back early, or just a friend visiting him.'

'Listen, I can hear voices. Look, look over there, two men in a big speedboat.'

'I wish these binoculars were infra-red so we could see everything.'

Toby snorts at me, 'Hey, Spence, why don't you use your *magic* tiger's eye to see who it is?'

I had *already* thought of that. 'Because the light is so brilliant they would be able to see us.'

Toby huffs to himself.

'They're getting closer to the island,' I say. We are both whispering now.

'Crikey, I think they really are trying to land here, Spence. Can you hear what they're saying?'

'Not above the noise of the outboard.'

'I think we should move back into the trees so they don't see us.'

We stay in the shadows of the trees, watching and trying to hear what they are saying. They definitely want to land here. They motor slowly along the shallows in front of the stony beach, where we had been fossil hunting during the afternoon.

I think they've just noticed Grandad's launch and *Splash* moored off the pier.

'What can they want at this time of night?'

'Maybe they want to steal Grandad's launch or *Splash*.'

'Don't say a word now, Spence, they are too close. Hold your breath.'

Suddenly the engine is switched off. Everything is deathly quiet, only broken by the heavy wash from their boat splashing against the shore and under the trees where we are now hiding. The muffled sound of voices and the crashing of oars fill the night air.

Toby has pushed me behind him so I can't see a thing now. He turns his head round and whispers.

'There are two men. They've tied their boat onto the pier next to *Splash*. They are coming ashore. Be really quiet, Spence, don't move. I don't like the look of them and they sound as rough as old boots.'

'Get the stuff, then. The shovel's in the back locker. Be quick about it and pass it up to me.'

'Who do you think those boats belong to?'

'I don't know. *Sir Francis Drake*?'

'I thought you said this was a deserted island?'

'Let's get on with our *business*. OK?'

'OK.'

'We've got our orders and you don't let the boss down, so let's get this hole dug and then we can bury the gear, because if we get caught with this we'll be looking at the inside of four grey walls for the next twenty years.'

Toby and I stare at each other. Blimey!

'We wouldn't have to do this if the boat meeting us hadn't broken her engine.'

'How long do you think it'll be before Metal Mickey fixes it?'

'God knows...'

'Where shall we dig the hole?'

'What about just up there, on the beach behind that tree?'

'OK.'

I can see the two men now as they are further up the beach. My eye seems to be getting used to the darkness. One of the men seems to be fat and the other one short and thin. I can't tell what their faces look like.

The short thin guy is digging the hole. The fat one is keeping a look out. What I don't understand is where Dad and Uncle Steven are. I can only suppose they're watching and listening too.

The two men place a big plastic container into the hole they have just dug before covering it over with sand.

'Where shall I put the shovel?'

'Hide it under those hanging branches the other side of the pier.'

'Oh no, Spence, they mean *here*. Quick, Spence, get back. Get back, quickly and don't say a word!'

State the blinkin' obvious, Toby, why don't you.

## Chapter 3

# *Kidnapped!*

Now I'm really scared, actually even more scared than I've ever felt before. Crikey, I think I need to have a poo! In fact I know I want a poo. I am really desperate for the toilet...

Toby suddenly puts his hand over my mouth, which startles me. Unfortunately I let out a rather loud blow-off – well, rather more a loud squeak than a blow. Toby is horrified.

'I'm so sorry, Toby, I really need to go for a poo.'

'Spence, be quiet. I covered your mouth to stop you making any noise. I didn't think I needed to cover your backside as well!'

I can see the pirates approaching quickly.

We are standing really, really still, holding our breath for as long as we can. Although I think Toby might be holding his breath for another reason...

They pass really close by. One of the men leans the shovel up against the big tree trunk in the middle.

They start to turn around and head back to the pier, when suddenly from nowhere we can hear Uncle Steven and Dad's voices heading this way. They appear to be chatting and not showing any signs of alarm.

'Check it out and don't use your gun unless you have to.'

The short thin guy pulls something out of his pocket.

'Toby, did you hear him say they've got a gun?'

'Yes. I think I saw it!'

'Me too.'

'What shall we do? We need to let Dad and Uncle Steven know they've got a gun.'

'Just stay hidden, but get ready to move... I don't know what to do!'

The darkness makes it hard to see where to put your feet. The branches and leaves have started to move and rustle with the breeze, brushing against my legs and face like creeping fingers and making me shiver all over.

Toby reaches out to grab my hand. I jump! It sort of makes me feel less brave and I want to call out to Dad, but something stops me.

We see that Dad and Uncle Steven have spotted the speedboat moored alongside *Splash* and that they are heading directly for the pier.

The pirates step from their cover into the open.

'Hi there, sorry to bother you mate...'

Uncle Steven looks quite angry. Please be careful Dad. Don't upset the nutter with the gun.

'Who the hell are you? And what do you want? Can't you read? This is a private Island and you're trespassing.'

Nice one, Uncle Steven.

Uncle Steven is much bigger than either of these two men. He has moved directly towards them.

'Yeah, sorry mate, we've run out of juice.'

'In both tanks? That's a bit unlikely.'

'Yeah, both... Well, it sounded like fuel...'

'I'll take a look for you.'

'That won't be necessary mate.'

Dad is staying well back, watching. The two men are now between Dad and Uncle Steven.

'Well, if it's lack of fuel, I'm sure I can give you enough petrol to get you back to wherever you came from. The fuel barge won't be open until 8.30 am and I'm sorry, mate, but you are not staying here for the night.'

Uncle Steven is heading along the pier as he's talking. I see the two men exchange glances.

Uncle Steven is now at the end of the pier, pulling in on the painter which is attached to their boat.

'What do you think you're doing, *mate*?'

'Just having a look to see if I can get it started. Checking whether it's fuel starvation or not.'

Uncle Steven is about to step into their boat from the end of the pier, when the man behind Uncle Steven pulls out a gun from his pocket and points it at the back of Uncle Steven's head!

'No you're not, mate. What a shame you're such a nosy *git*. Now get away from the boat and join your brother. That is your brother isn't it? Or are you just wearing matching orange bubble wigs 'cos the circus is in town?

The other pirate is laughing.

'Oh yeah, I forgot to mention. Try anything stupid and *I'll blow your brains out!'*

The other man is pointing his gun at Dad. Well, today has certainly taken a turn for the worse! Dad is like a statue. Uncle Steven does as the man says. He walks slowly away from the end of the pier back towards Dad.

Toby and I are clinging tightly together. My heart is pounding. The coldness I felt earlier has now gone.

As Dad and Uncle Steven stand alongside each other, one of the pirates raises his gun, waving it towards them, shouting to them to empty their pockets out and take off their sailing jackets for them to check. After a few minutes searching through their pockets they throw back their coats. Then the fat guy hurls two things into the harbour. I'm not sure, but I think it was their mobile phones.

The two men make Dad and Uncle Steven walk in front with their hands above their heads. They follow a few feet behind them, still holding their guns up. I think they want to know where our camp is. I lose sight of them as they head towards the dunes.

Toby and I wait for some minutes, before we speak.

'Shall I use my *tiger's eye* now, Toby, to see where they've gone?'

Toby looks at me as if I am mad. 'This isn't the time for your silly imaginary games now, Spence. This is serious.'

'Well, what now, then?' I whisper to Toby.

'Warn Ben. Get some help.'

Toby starts to head through the trees towards the direction of the camp.

I gently pull at Toby's hand.

'Toby, I think we should head for the safety of our lookout tree and make a proper plan. If we rush after Dad and Uncle Steven we might all be caught.'

'OK Spence, let's try and get to our tree.'

We carefully and quietly make our way through the darkness towards our lookout tree.

Sitting up in the tree at night, we can't see very much. The lights all around Poole Harbour look pretty and we can even see the lights on Furzey Island. And that reminds me, there *is* help very near by, we just *have* to reach it.

'Toby, what shall we do? It will be difficult looking for Ben in the dark. We can't call out his name or we might give ourselves away, and for all we know, he might already be a prisoner too.'

'Well, we must decide how we can get some help.'

'I've got an idea. Why don't we take Grandad's launch, row her clear of the island, then start her engine and go back to Poole Yacht Club and get us some help? I can use the VHF radio and call *Mayday*.'

'Nice idea, Spence, just one problem – Dad's got the engine key with him!'

'Yes, I know, but Grandad showed me how to start the engine using a special handle he keeps in one of his stern lockers. I've seen him do it. He even let me have a go once.'

'Yeah? And did you get it started?'

'Well, no...' Toby groans. '...but I'm older now and bigger and I know how to decompress the engine and everything, and if Ben's with us he's fifteen and he'll be able to do it.'

'That sounds like we might have a chance, but what about navigating in the dark?'

'I've thought of that. As long as we stay between the red and green posts we'll be OK. That can't be too hard, they have lights on the top flashing red and green and my special tiger's eye will help guide me.'

Toby groans again. *'Spence, you haven't got a magic tiger's eye.* My Mum told me. You made it up in your mind to help you get over your accident or something like that.'

I want to take my patch off and show Toby, but ... well, I just decide not to.

'But, Toby, once we see the lights of Poole Quay, we're home and dry and the tide is still coming in for a few hours. So even if things go pear-shaped, we'll not get washed out to sea for a while!'

Toby does not seem impressed by any of this. 'We should just wait till daylight, Spence.'

'But we haven't got the *time*! Plus we'll be spotted during the day, and I don't know about you but I'm not sure I can spend a whole night stuck up this tree.'

Toby is nodding his head. Swimming trunks and tree bark are not a good combination for your crown jewels!

'I agree with that. If we can get back to camp first we'll need to get some money to call the police when we land and then we'll...'

'Be quiet, someone's coming!'

We hear the sound of breaking twigs on the ground, and then heavy breathing.

Toby and I once again try not to move a muscle or make a single sound. I am too afraid to look below. I close my eye really tightly. Someone or something has stopped really close to this tree.

# Chapter 4

# *The Rescue*

'Boo! That spooked you! What a great hiding place. I wondered where you'd got to.'

It's Ben. He's right under our tree looking up at us. I'm trying so hard not to let Ben and Toby know how scared I am. My heart is about to escape from my chest!

'Great tree, can I come up?'

'Yes, quickly. But keep your voice down.'

'Are you hiding from Dad and Uncle Ronnie?'

'No!'

'Well, why all the whispering? Who are you hiding from?'

'Where have you been for the past hour, Ben?'

'I had to go for a poo. Dad told me to go as far away from his tent as possible. So I did. So come on, why are we all whispering?'

'This might sound a bit far-fetched, Ben, but I promise you it did happen.'

Toby tells Ben all about the last hour.

'You've just *made that all up!*'

'No, Ben, we haven't. Please believe us, that's why we were hiding in the tree and too scared to

39

call out to you. We thought you were one of the pirates.'

'I'm still not sure you two aren't just winding me up. I'm going back to camp to see for myself.'

'*No!*' Toby and I shout out in the loudest whisper of all time.

'Please don't go, Ben, please don't go. Please, please...' I've started to blub like a little girl. How embarrassing.

'OK, Spence, it's OK, I believe you, I believe you. Anything to stop you crying.'

We explain to Ben how we plan to take Grandad's launch to get help. Ben agrees it's a good plan. At first Ben suggests taking *Splash*, the sailing dingy. But the lack of wind added to our appalling night-time navigation skills could get us all in a whole lot more trouble. We all decide to keep to the original plan.

Ben also thinks the men with the guns are smugglers and they are hiding drugs on the island for fear of their boat being searched by the Customs and Excise people, who have the right to board any vessel if they suspect it of smuggling. Ben says they use dogs to sniff out the drugs.

At last we decide to start our rescue mission. We quietly climb down from the tree.

After a few minutes back on the ground I feel my stomach churning over and remember how desperately I need the loo.

'Ben, before we go, can you tell me where you went to the toilet?'

'Why?'

'It's just I'm busting for a poo.'

'Come on then, Spence, I'll show you.'

Ben takes us towards the other side of the island, near where Uncle Steven said there was sinking sand and mud.

This is quite a long walk to go to the toilet. It's taking quite a lot of effort not to let the turtle's head escape from my bottom, which is making us all laugh, but walking in the opposite direction to where the smugglers are feels quite good too.

At last Ben stops. 'There, under those sticks and leaves.' Ben points to a large bush a few feet in front of us.

'How did you manage to find your way back here in the dark, Ben?'

'Easy, I took a bearing using my compass and then calculated a reciprocal course.'

Toby and I nod our heads in approval of Ben's wise manoeuvre.

Anyway, I feel an awful lot better, until I realise there is a serious lack of toilet paper available! Doh!

'Ben, I don't suppose you've got any toilet...'

And as I turn round, Ben produces a wad of folded toilet paper from his fleece pocket, letting it drop from his hand like a streamer.

'Thanks, Ben.'

Toby has decided all this toilet business has made him want to go too, so we retreat out of harm's way (as Ben says).

Ben makes us all laugh, saying it's a shame we can't replace their buried treasure with our big pile of buried treasure! That will confuse the poor sniffer dogs!

I feel much safer now Ben is here. He is always kind-hearted, and makes me laugh too. But I can't stop worrying about Dad and Uncle Steven.

We creep as close to the camp as we dare, once more using Ben's hand-held compass in the dark, giving us a perfect course back. He's so clever to think of that.

Although it is dark, I can clearly see the silhouette of the tents against the water. There is no one about. There are no lights and no sounds.

We watch for a short while.

'Maybe they're in the tent. Or maybe they've taken Dad and Uncle Steven off the island. Shall we check the boats are still here?'

'No, we're wasting time; they've probably taken them up to the house and tied them up.'

'Well, I think the camp is safe. Toby, you go to your tent and get yours and Spencer's oilskins and don't forget your wallet. We still need to call the police from the payphone as soon as we land. I'll go and get my stuff from Dad's tent and some food and water. Spence, you keep a lookout. Make an owl noise if you hear or see anything.'

'I'm not very good at hoots through my hands like you Ben, but I can make this noise, *HoooooT HoooooT*, will that do?'

'You sound like an *ill, asthmatic budgie*, Spence.

But unless these blokes are keen ornithologists we'll be OK!'

We all quietly laugh.

Ben and Toby slip off towards the tents whilst I stay crouched low on the ground, looking all around as far as I can in the dark. It seems ages and then Toby appears with our oilskins and his wallet. We stay together watching out for Ben. Then Toby decides to go and see what is taking Ben so long.

'I'm going to give Ben a hand. The water bottles are really heavy.'

'Don't you think we should wait here for him?'

'Look, I won't be long, Spence, I promise!'

'OK. I'll move back further into the trees and wait for you there.'

I gather all the oilskin jackets and trousers up in my arms and I make a quick dash for further cover into the trees. I slip on my trousers and top jacket, feeling instantly warmer. I put Toby's wallet safely away in the zip-up pocket of my oilskin jacket.

My life-jacket feels rather tight now with this lot on.

This is like torture, waiting here for Ben and now Toby. Come on, come on...

But nothing, I mean *nothing* happens. It's like they've both disappeared into the Bermuda Triangle, but that's situated in the Pacific, just to the east of Miami... Oh my God, my over-active brain is even beginning to bore my own pants off!

I can't believe Ben and Toby are taking so long. I mean, why would they? Just to scare me? Well, it's working! What *is* keeping them?

Ah! A dark figure has appeared from Dad's tent. I think it must be Ben... Wait... *No!* It's one of the men, followed by Dad and Uncle Steven, who have got their hands tied up behind their backs. It looks like they've been gagged too.

A few moments later a smaller figure appears from the tent. It's Toby and now Ben, both gagged, with their hands tied behind their backs.

The other man appears from the tent. He is still pointing his gun at Dad and Uncle Steven!

Lying flat on the ground, trying to keep my high-visibility oilskins and life-jacket out of sight, with my head craned up just enough to see the six figures in front of the tent, I can hear quite clearly what the men are saying. They must think they have caught everyone because they are making no efforts to prevent detection. I wonder how long they had waited in the tent to trap us.

The short thin man is moving around, pointing his gun at Uncle Steven and Dad as he speaks.

'I'm taking these kids to the house up there on the hill. Any trouble and your kids will get it. Do I make myself clear?'

Dad and Uncle Steven appear to nod. I think Ben and Toby must be terrified.

I want to help, but I don't know how I can. I

watch helplessly as the man leads Ben and Toby away towards the house. I can see Toby looking over his shoulder back towards the woods where he knows I am.

I keep watching until I lose Ben and Toby in the darkness. Then I fix my one-eyed stare across at the beach where Dad and Uncle Steven are being held hostage.

It seems forever before the man orders Dad and Uncle Steven to go back into the tent. Poor Dad, he can hardly get back to his feet with his hands tied behind his back. Uncle Steven tries to help Dad. Finally Dad is back on his feet, walking back into the tent. As they disappear my eye starts to fill up with tears, my nose now full of thick snot. I gulp air through my mouth to compensate for my blocked nostrils. Please will someone come and help me, help my Dad...

The next move even surprises me!

I quickly and quietly jump to my feet and hurry through the trees back to the stony beach, where these evil men had arrived less than two hours earlier.

I look out across the pier. I see *Splash* and Grandad's launch safely moored and the smugglers' boat between *Splash* and the pier.

I run across to the place where the men buried their container.

*'Yes, well, I'm going to take your buried treasure as you've taken my Dad and Uncle Steven and cousins, and see how you like that!'*

Running back to the trees, I grab the spade they had hidden earlier and dig up a large waterproof container. I carefully fill the hole back in. The container is really heavy and certainly doesn't look much like treasure.

I take the spade back to the trees and carry the container to the edge of the pier. Pulling on the mooring line attached to *Splash*, I bring her alongside the pier. I climb quietly into her using the mast to steady myself. I drop the container onto the deck. I release her mooring line just enough so I can reach Grandad's launch. I still leave her secured to the pier. I don't want to cast her adrift.

I slowly pull myself along with the ships oars until I'm close enough to come alongside. *Splash* is quite frisky with the fast tide running under her. I quickly heave the container into the launch. Leaping over the gunwales of both boats with a frankly dangerous scissors jump was a bit tricky and potentially fatal for my crown jewels, but I landed safely enough.

*Splash* is quickly swept down tide and back towards the island on her extra-long mooring line. When she reaches the end of her line she sort of gives a little jerk and then her bow gently swings into the flow of the tide.

Now to find the starting handle! The last place I remember seeing it was in one of the aft lockers. Pulling them open I rummage about in the dark. There are all sorts of tools but *no* starting handle.

But I have made enough space to hide the plastic container right at the back, just in case.

I can't find it! Come on Grandad, where did you hide it?

Nothing in this locker...

Nothing in this locker... Come on...

The third locker is tightly packed, but yes, I pull out Grandad's old tool box. Quickly pulling it open, almost right on top is the starting handle.
　Taking off the lid to the engine box is easy enough. Looking down into the engine in the darkness is not. I have to familiarise myself with what I could remember. In daylight it was complicated enough, but now it's impossible. I look around. Is it safe enough to use my tiger's eye? Keeping my head down, I take my patch off.

*A sharp blade of light pierces the blackness. The deck of Grandad's launch is now brilliantly illuminated.*

Waiting a few seconds for my human eye to acclimatise to the light, I am able to locate the starting handle, and using all the strength I can muster begin to push and pull the handle up. Gritting my teeth so hard, increasing the speed of the turning until I'm moving the handle really, really fast. Then the 'pop pop splutter' of the engine begins.
　'Yes!'

I take the tiller and gently steer the launch away from Monkey Island, moving into deeper water and head for the closest channel mark.

I pop my patch back on. I'm like a short, freaky, one-eyed superhero! I start to hum the theme tune to James Bond.

I want to go really fast, but just trying to pick my way from post to post in the darkness is hard enough at slow speed. I try to find my way round to the corner of the island, then passing to the west of Green Island and Furzey Island.

Suddenly the very welcome sight of the Poole Ferry terminal and the lights from Poole Quay are over in the far distance. This makes me feel much safer. I'm going to phone the police and Mum and Jimmy when I get to Poole Yacht Club.

I'll be back soon, Dad. Hold on. Just hold on…

It's getting quite chilly now.

The water is deeper now and I feel colder as the wind picks up and the water gets choppier. I accelerate the throttle, pushing Grandad's launch hard and sending up a cold icy spray of water into my face.

I'm going to try and use the VHF radio as soon as I'm clear of Brownsea Island.

Slowing down again, I pick my way through the moored boats off Pottery pier in Maryland. I wish there was a boat I recognised. I steer slowly through the Wych Channel which at last opens back up into Wills Cut. I feel the tide becoming much stronger as I clear Brownsea Island.

I can see straight down the harbour now. There are lots of lights when I look right towards Sandbanks, but looking left towards Arne it seems very dark and very scary.

## Chapter 5

## *Mayday*

I open the port forward locker and turn Grandad's VHF radio on. I tune into Channel 16.

Although I am not supposed to use this, it is an emergency. I hold down the Speak button.

'Mayday, Mayday, Mayday.
'This is Grandad's launch. Grandad's launch.
'I am in Wills Cut heading to Poole Yacht Club.
'It's Spencer Drew.
'The pirates have got my Dad, Uncle Steven, Ben and Toby.
'They're prisoners on Monkey Island.
'I've taken the pirates' buried treasure.
'Please help me.
'Mayday, Mayday, Mayday.
'Oh yes ... over.'

I'm not really sure what happens next. I think I'll wait for five minutes then try again if they don't...

'Mayday Grandad's launch.
'This is Portland Coastguard. Portland Coastguard.

'Received Mayday.
'Launching helicopter.
'Over.'

Ruddy hell (as Jimmy would say, although I'm not allowed to swear), it worked!

I wonder if I should say anything else. I suppose they'll ask if they want something.

What's that? I can hear the sound of a speedboat approaching. I look over my shoulder and see one heading right for me.

No prizes for guessing what boat it is!

I push the throttle full on. Grandad's launch is going full steam ahead but it's no match for the speedboat. I turn hard to port, paying almost no attention to the channel marks. I think I'm heading towards Arne.

I grab the VHF handset and press the Speak button.

'Mayday, Mayday. Help!
'It's Spencer again. They're trying to kill me!
'I could *really* do with some help now!
'The speedboat is chasing me.
'Spencer Drew is heading towards Arne.
'Help!
'Mayday. Mayday.'

I throw down the handset and try to concentrate on helming Grandad's launch at full speed. The water is really choppy. I think it's because I'm over the shallows. I attempt to keep my bearings but the speedboat is right behind me.

I bet they've discovered I've taken their container. Well, they're not getting it back until they let my Dad, Uncle Steven, Ben and Toby go!

Please, please, hurry up helicopter.

The speedboat is now parallel to Grandad's launch. I push the tiller hard to starboard but it's such a tight turn at this speed I can feel the launch bury her nose deep into the large stern wave, tipping her port gunwale right into the drink and almost capsizing! The water spews over the side...

The man in the speedboat looks rather surprised at my spectacular manoeuvre; mind you, not as surprised as I am.

He's alongside me now!
  *'Captain Birdseye, stop the boat!'*
  'No!'

Slowing the launch right down, I push the tiller a little more gently to port, tacking away from the speedboat. I don't have a plan any more, but I think I'd like to live another day!
  *'You little twit, you can't get away from me. Just hand over the stuff and I'll let you live!'*

Suddenly I spot the navigation lights of a fast-approaching air-sea rescue helicopter. Thank God!

* * *

The helicopter is hovering right above us. Suddenly a blinding light beams down from above.

The man in the speedboat tacks away to starboard, and the helicopter follows keeping the bright light fixed on his boat.

The man takes out his gun. I hit the deck really quickly thinking he is going to fire at me!

*Bang!*

Luckily for me, he's fired at the helicopter, and thankfully appears to have missed. Instantly the helicopter turns away and disappears into the night.

'Come back, come back!' I shout.

But it doesn't look as if it's coming back.

'*Right, Captain Birdseye, it's just you and me; stop the boat and hand over the stuff.*'

'No! Never!'

I push the throttle onto full power and head away from the man.

Quickly he is back in pursuit.

A sudden impact throws me over the engine box, catching my right shoulder really hard on the wooden post in the centre. The speedboat has rammed the back of the launch. I pick myself up and grab hold of the tiller.

Again he attempts to ram me. I push the tiller hard to port, just cutting back the revs as she turns. The speedboat only just misses me. He turns to make another attack.

By this time I have picked up quite a lick of speed and as she is turning I ram the stern of the speedboat, catching her outboard quite hard!

Heading away as fast as I can I take a quick glance over my shoulder, only to see an extraordinary sight! The speedboat is going round and round in circles, whilst the man is being thrown around the boat attempting to get to the engine!

I must have bent the rudder when I rammed the back of his outboard.

Now heading towards Poole Quay as fast as I can, as the spinning speedboat is blocking my entrance to the Yacht Club.

The quay looks really quiet. Where is everyone? I pass the new visitor's yacht haven. It looks full of boats but there are no people.

I steer Grandad's launch away from the quayside, dropping back towards the new visitors' haven. I spot some concrete steps rising up from the water alongside the quay.

I bring the launch up to the steps, leaving the engine ticking over in neutral. I secure a bow line to the large black mooring cleats. I climb the Fish Shamble Steps and take one last look at the launch. I pass the little trip boat kiosk and cross the road toward the amusement arcade.

This is like a ghost town. Not one single car, motorbike or person has come past. I suppose everyone's gone to bed.

Something doesn't seem quite right. I just can't cope with any more surprises.

## Chapter 6

# *999*

Just in front of the amusement arcade there are two telephone boxes. I reach into the inside pocket of my oilskin jacket to check I've still got Toby's wallet.

I take a quick look up and down the deserted quay. Spooky.

I decide to use the second telephone box as it's hidden by the first one (just in case the man with the gun has followed me).

The door is almost too heavy to pull open. I can only use my left arm properly. My right arm and shoulder are still sore where I bashed it in the launch.

The door closes quickly behind me, nearly knocking me over as it shuts. There is at least a light on in here so I can hunt for some ten and twenty pence pieces to phone the police and Mum and Jimmy.

Good. Toby's got loads of change. I carefully tip out the contents.

'Toby you idiot, this is all euros!'

There's not one *sodding* ten pence piece!

'*Merci beaucoup*, Toby!'

I try ringing 999; maybe they can ring me back. Nine, nine, nine…

'Which service do you require: Police, fire or ambulance?'

'Hello, I'm Spencer Drew, I'm calling from a phone box on Poole Quay and I want the police to help me. I haven't got any money. The rescue helicopter has flown away and I'm all alone. Please can you send help, I need to get Dad, Uncle Steven, Ben and Toby off Monkey Island.'

The lady on the phone asks me to wait.

'Hello, Spencer, how are you?'

'I'm fine, who are you?'

'I'm Chief Inspector Abbey Brook.'

'Are you a real Chief Inspector?'

'Yes, Spencer. I'm here to help your father. There are already police officers on Poole Quay.'

'Where? I haven't seen anyone.'

'They are going to protect you from the man who shot at the helicopter. Spencer, how many other people have guns?'

'Well, I think the thin man on Monkey Island has one, he's still keeping Dad and the others prisoners. The thin man spoke about a boss. He's not on Monkey Island but on a boat somewhere in Poole Harbour. They also talked about a man they called Metal Mickey who is on another boat somewhere, but that boat has a broken engine, which Metal Mickey is supposed to fix. That's all the people I heard them talk about.'

'Well done, Spencer, you have been incredibly clever and very brave. Do you think you could be brave just a little bit longer to help us rescue your family and arrest these men?'

'Yes, what do I have to do?'

'I would like you to go back to your Grandad's launch and return to Monkey Island.'

'What if I get caught by that man with the gun?'

'That won't be a problem, just go along with them. However, I can tell you there are already several armed policemen on Monkey Island. We now need to set a trap to catch the men without arousing suspicion.'

'What sort of trap? Like in Scooby Doo when Shaggy and Scooby are used as decoys to trap the villains?'

'Well, sort of, but this is a trick to get the men to follow you to a special place on Monkey Island where they think you may have hidden their container. Can you think of anywhere on the island that would be a suitable place to set a trap?'

'Well, there was our lookout tree, but even better than that, over the north side of the island, there's this bush where ... well, where Ben, Toby and I went for a poo! It's just that because Ben used his compass, he was able to navigate there and back in the dark, so you see I could easily find it if I had a compass. I remember the bearings were 350 degrees north there and the reciprocal course back to our camp was 170 degrees south. I can work out a reciprocal course by adding or subtracting 180. It's just a sum!'

'Spencer, that sounds perfect.'

'But does that mean I have to bury the container and let them find it?'

'Not exactly, Spencer. We have already taken the container away.'

'But how did you know where to look?'

'Our sniffer dog Rex found it straight away.'

'Cool! I bet he'd have no difficulty finding the exact place I'm talking about too! Although he might not survive his mission long enough to...'

Abbey coughs.

'Spencer, I want you to try and trick the men into believing you buried their container where you described. We will set up an ambush.'

'That sounds like a good plan, but I'll need a compass to help me find my way.'

'One of our officers has already left one next to the VHF radio. Is there anything else you want to ask or tell me before you leave?'

'Well, I'd really like to phone my Mum and Jimmy but I don't have any ten or twenty-pence pieces.'

'Your mum and stepdad are already on their way.'

'Are you sure? How do you know their number?'

'The moment you called Mayday, Portland Coastguard immediately contacted the police and traced them. They will be here very shortly, I promise. One more thing, Spencer, it may not be wise to use the VHF radio.'

'Oh, have I got Grandad into trouble?'

'No, Spencer, it may be that the men on Monkey Island are listening to our transmissions.'

'I understand. Shall I go back to Grandad's launch now?'

'Yes please, Spencer. And remember, we will be

looking after you. So even if you can't see us, we can see you.'

I hang the phone up.

I think I can hear the helicopter coming back.

*Smash!*

As I turn my head to face the opening door of the phone box, the man with the gun is right in front of me. I back up against the phone. The ugly fat man presses his face right up against the glass door, banging the gun hard against the glass, making me jump back hard against the phone set!
   *'You, Captain Birdseye, get out of there now.'*

Crud! (I think in the circumstances a swear word might be appropriate.)

A flash of blinding light pierces through the glass phone box. It's almost too bright to keep my eye open. The helicopter must be really near. It can't be more than a few feet away. The noise and wind from the down-draught is incredible and very scary.
   The ugly man bangs his gun against the phone box in anger.
   *'I'll get you later, Cyclops!'*
   He lets go his grip on the phone box and sort of twists away with a bandy-legged walk towards Poole Bridge. The helicopter follows.
   I think I'm going to make a run for it too!

I budge the door with my right shoulder. Big

mistake! I feel very dizzy and fall to my knees from the awful pain in my shoulder.

Remember not to do that again! Up on my feet, I'm out and already running across the road, heading for Fish Shamble Steps, where Grandad's launch is still ticking over.

I throw the mooring line into the bottom of the launch and jump into the boat. The helicopter is heading towards Poole lifting bridge, his bright light searching all over the empty black water.

I head once again back towards Wills Cut.

Whilst focused on my mission, the threat of the vile man catching me up fills me with terror.

I grab the compass which Abbey has left me and tie it around my neck with a piece of line.

... Too scared to even look over my shoulder to see if I'm being followed ...

# Chapter 7

# *The Trap*

For the first time in ages I can take a look at my watch. Its 1.30 am (or tomorrow morning already).

I can see Monkey Island a little better against the night sky and crouch down low into a sort of gnome position to keep warm.

The wind is coming from the south and has strengthened quite a bit since I left Poole Quay. My shoulder is sore and I feel so tired...

I pull out the hood on my oilskin jacket and fasten the toggle as tightly as I can to keep my head warm.

I feel scared and lonely, but I need to stay *sharp* to win this battle!

I make sure the anchor is ready to drop over, when I get close enough...

Oh, crud, I've just realized, I'm going to have to get wet! I can't bring Grandad's launch in too close and this time I don't have *Splash* to get ashore. I'll have to keep my oilskins dry, so I'd better slip them off when I've anchored and carry them above my head. Then I'll have something dry to wear to keep me warm.

I'm getting really close to Monkey Island. I'd better cut down the engine speed and be as quiet as I can.

I begin to weave my way through the narrow channel, which at low water is almost unnavigable.

I remove my oilskins to keep them dry and save time... Oh crud! I've been foiled by my own stupid granny knot on my hood. As though life wasn't complicated enough, I've now got myself trapped in my own oilskin jacket!

Steering Grandad's launch through South Deep with the tide running away is becoming increasingly difficult (especially with this crazy noose stuck around my neck). Even with the engine in neutral, the launch is still slipping through the channel too quickly. Grandad's launch is turning side on and the tiller won't turn her head around. If I don't slow her down soon and get control of her steerage, I'll be past Monkey Island and stuck in the mud over in Newtown Bay!

I try putting her astern, which slows me down. I can see the wooden pier on Monkey Island where Grandad's launch was previously at anchor. It's behind me. I'm going too fast!

'Doh!'

Grandad's launch has suddenly lurched back sending a sharp pain through my shoulder.

Run aground! There must be a big lump of mud

on the edge of the channel! Increasing the revs just churns up loads of mud and weed.

I'm not going anywhere now. 'Accept and move on', that's what Jimmy would say. I'm sorry Grandad; I think she'll be OK. If the police are watching me I'm sure they'll keep an eye on her too. Some help they are!

The thought of turning the engine off is quite scary. But I can't leave her ticking over forever.

I pull out the decompression switch, which is followed by an eerie silence.

The silence makes the darkness seem darker and the night air feels even colder.

I heave the anchor towards the shore on Monkey Island, but for all my effort (and the horrendous pain in my shoulder), I only bring it about two feet away from the launch. At this rate I'll be finished by a week next Thursday.

Oh yeah, and I try one last failed attempt to wrench the hood off my head. Seizing the oilskin trousers I removed earlier and gathering up my jacket around my neck as high as I can without garroting myself with the drawstring (successfully), I reluctantly resign myself to a temporary incarceration in my red hood.

With no more time to mess about I brace myself for the one-armed, one-eyed swim ashore.

Slipping over the gunwale and into the cold water takes my breath away.

I *have* to keep moving forward, but as I wade

through the water with my hands above my head holding up my oilskins to keep dry, I already feel my centre of balance leaning a little too far forward and all of a sudden the floor disappears... Whoa!

Yes, I am completely soaked; I've even managed to drink some of Poole Harbour in too... I'll probably grow my eye back now!

My oilskin jacket is laying spread out on the surface of the water, half turned around on my head covering my right eye. I grab my rapidly sinking trousers and start swimming towards the pier (when I say swimming I really mean lying on my back floating in the direction of the shore). My sore shoulder and my oilskin jacket are doing their best to slow me down. Looking on the bright side, at least my life-jacket is keeping me afloat.

Somehow I have managed to reach the shore. My eye patch has been dragged onto my forehead like Cyclops, the one-eyed mythical giant. Unbelievably I spot *Splash*, my Mirror dingy. She has drifted back to shore. Crikey, it looks as if my bad luck virus is wearing off!

I walk *Splash* along the shallows, shortening her mooring line to keep her just afloat off the pier.

I slip off my life-jacket and stow it in *Splash* as far out of sight as I can. My wet oilskin jacket is still stuck on my head. I bet James Bond never had this sort of problem with his toggle and oilskins!

It's time to find Dad, Uncle Steven, Ben and Toby.

I walk straight through the trees to the beach.

The camp looks empty; but I'm not falling for that old chestnut again!

No sign of *Dougal* or the speedboat. I wonder if the police have already arrested them and rescued everyone.

I head towards Dad's tent and decide to adopt a slightly bolder more direct approach!

'Come out; come out, wherever you are!'

*Silence.*

I go slightly crazy and burst through the entrance of the tent, like some mad Kung Fu kid. Not a sausage.

I check all the tents (with the same mad Kung Fu crazy routine).

*Nothing.*

Well, now to get this wretched hood off of my head! Over by the barbecue is a plastic box of cutlery. One of the kitchen knives does the trick and relieves me of my oilskin jacket.

'Oh crud! I've cut the string on my lucky stone as well!'

*I'll keep it with me, Dad, I promise. I'll tie another knot. I'm great at tying knots that won't come undone!*

I return to my tent to find my wetsuit. I put it on. This will cover all eventualities whether I get wet or stay dry and it will keep me warm. I hide my oilskins under the groundsheet, so nobody can tell I've been here.

Using the compass I make my way through the dunes and then through the woods. Eventually I come to the edge of an area of open grass, a little overgrown, stopping only for a moment to catch my breath. I'm across the grass in two shakes of a lamb's tail.

The grass leads up to a tall brick wall. I walk along by the wall for a short while, passing an old greenhouse packed full of overgrown tomato plants. Walking out and round the greenhouse, a narrow shingle path leads off into the darkness. The path leads to an old wooden gate.

The gate isn't locked. Looking furtively around, I push it open and step inside...

Sure enough it *is* the house. Closing the gate behind me as quietly as I can, I approach what looks like the back of the house as I can't see any front door, just a set of French windows and two other windows one either side of the house. There are no lights on.

I walk along the edge of the grass. Ducking down low, I stoop past the first window, lifting my head up to see if I can see anything. I can't see any sign of life. Getting closer this time, I press my face up against one of the small glass panels in the French windows.

One of the panes of glass near to the handle has been smashed. The handle turns easily. Pulling the French windows open I push aside the curtains. I enter a darkened room.

An owl hoots and I nearly wee myself. Calm down, Spencer!

*       *       *

At least my black wetsuit hides me well in the dark.

I really do feel like James Bond, except I don't have a dinner jacket and bow tie underneath my wetsuit, just a pair of stinky trunks!

I feel my way across the room, eventually finding a light switch that doesn't work.

Is it safe to use my tiger's eye I wonder? No, the light might be seen by the wrong people and give me away. What I really need is a dimmer switch control... I'll mention that to Q next time I see him.

The room leads into a hallway with stairs. I check all the downstairs rooms first. Tripping and bumping my way through two more rooms downstairs, I tip toe up the stairs.

Am I alone?

This all seems a bit pointless, but I may as well check it out. Turning right at the top of the stairs I enter the first door on my right. It's quite a big room.

It really whiffs of something familiar... What is it? The harbour!

I can make out the window as there is some brightness breaking through the curtains. It must be getting light outside.

'Hhhmm, Hhmmmm!'

What was that? From inside this room, there is a sort of moaning noise as though someone was hurt.

'Who's there?'

'Hhhmmm, mmm, hh, hh, errrr!'

Turning round, the groaning noise is coming from the other side of the room, and who ever it is, they are not moving.

*I have no choice. I take off my patch and the beam of light from my tiger's eye blasts out, striking the corner of the room.*

I gasp at what I see!

# Chapter 8

# *Dawn Breaks*

It is Ben and Toby! And they don't look in a good state. In fact Toby's going a bit bonkers. They are both gagged and bound and it looks really uncomfortable.

'Hold on, hold on, I'm coming.'

I quickly rip off the large plaster which is covering Toby's mouth.

Of course, under normal circumstances I would have really enjoyed doing that, but right now it was joining a long list of unbelievable things I have had to do.

'Aaahh!'

'Sorry... Am I glad to see you two. How come Ben's so quiet? Is he asleep?'

'Oh, Spencer, I think Ben's dead...'

Toby is in floods of tears. I can't understand what he is trying to tell me. Then he puts his hand on my tiger's eye.

'It's real...'

*Well, of course it's real*, I think to myself. I pull the patch back over my eye.

'It's real.'

I think Toby is in shock! He looks over towards Ben.

I leap over to Ben and instinctively rip the plaster from his mouth, but no sound comes from his lips. Ben is still unconscious (a bit like I was when I was in hospital). I gently lay my head on his chest to listen to his heart, and hold my hand close to his mouth and nose.

'I don't think he's dead, Toby, he's really warm and his heart is still beating.'

'Are you sure, Spence?' Toby whines and sobs.

'Quite sure.'

'Untie me, Spence, let me see.'

'What happened to Ben?'

'Show me he's not dead, Spencer, show me how you can tell? I want to hear his heart beating.'

I untie Ben and show Toby (who is still sobbing), how to listen to Ben's heart.

'We should put Ben on his side. I think it's called the recovery position. It will make him get better, I promise.'

'Do you really think so? It's my entire fault Spencer, if I hadn't made a run for it, Ben wouldn't have got hurt.'

Toby is sobbing really loudly. I put my arms around him.

'Whatever happened, Toby? You both did what you had to do. You didn't hurt Ben. Whoever did this to Ben is the bad guy. Please don't worry. Ben's too big and tough and Mum always says sleep is the best cure. So we'll let him sleep.'

'I can't help blaming myself for what happened to Ben. Earlier we had all been kept together in the kitchen. Dad and Uncle Ronnie were really tied up tightly; we only had our hands tied to begin with. When the fat man came back to the house, he was really angry. Anyway they argued a lot but then the thin man had a call on his mobile and they went into the other room to talk. I overheard the thin man tell the fat man, they were bringing the boat over to Goat Horn Point.

Then the thin man marched our dads out after untying their feet. And he was holding a gun at your dad's head. 'A few minutes after they left, I stupidly got up when the fat man was looking out of the kitchen window and made a dash for the kitchen door. Everything happened so quickly, the man had turned around before I had a chance to reach the door. I didn't even have enough time to open the door. Ben must have seen him coming after me and put himself between me and the fat man.

'The man was so angry. Ben shouted back at the man to leave me alone. The man turned on Ben, raised his gun and brought it down hard onto the back of Ben's head. The thing is, if only I hadn't tried to escape, Ben would have been OK. I feel so sick inside.'

'What happened then?'

'Well, Ben was very quiet for a while, dazed. But he still sheltered me from the fat man. It seemed ages before Ben stood upright. Then he started throwing up and holding his head and all the time the fat man was still shouting at us to get over there, do this, do that. Ben steadied himself and kept me close by his side; although I think he was more leaning on me by the time we got to the top of the stairs. 'The man pushed us into this bedroom, then gagged our mouths with parcel tape and bound our feet and hands. He left, and then sometime later you turned up.'

Toby sniffed and sobbed between his words.

'Well, Toby, the fat man was angry because I damaged the back of his outboard and he nearly caught me again on the quay when I called the police for help.'

'You managed to get to Poole Quay all on your own?'

'I used Grandad's VHF radio and sent out a Mayday call!'

'Well done, Spencer.'

'Don't worry, Toby, somewhere on this island there are lots of police waiting to ambush these men and rescue us. In fact they may have already caught them.'

'I don't think so, Spencer.'

'There really are policemen here, Toby, I promise...'

'But Spencer, when I was listening to the men arguing, they warned everyone to stay away from Monkey Island or they'd start to shoot the hostages! I thought they were bluffing until Ben got clouted with his gun. Anyway I thought you were listening in too, you'd have heard that message on Grandad's VHF radio.'

'No! I should have left it on, but Abbey said not to use the radio as the men could hear me, so I didn't and very stupidly switched it off!'

'Who the hell's Abbey?'

'She's a police inspector friend of mine. It's too complicated to explain it all now, just *trust me* Toby.'

Toby stares at me for a few seconds.

'Do you know what they were going to do with our dads? And why they didn't take you two?'

'I don't know the answer to either of those questions, Spencer. I guess they needed hostages, probably to negotiate their escape or to get their drugs back. I think they took our dads because keeping them tied up was better than risking them escaping and coming after them. After all, both our dads are over six foot and pretty tough.'

'That's true.'

I pull off my rucksack and offer Toby a much-needed drink. I find a packet of squashed crisps in there too.

As I pull open the crisp packet we suddenly turn to Ben as he rolls onto his back, lifts up his right arm and clutches his head.

'Oh my head...'

'Ben, Ben, are you OK?'

'Do I look OK?'

I think Ben is being *ironic*. My older sister is *ironic* all the time.

'You don't look OK at all.'

'Well, I'm not, I'm hungry and I can smell salt and vinegar crisps!'

Toby and I just look at each other, both smiling the biggest smile we've ever smiled at each other, with our eyes filling with tears.

'Ben, you really scared us, I thought you were dead!'

'I don't *feel* dead. When did you get here, Spencer? And what's happened to Dad and Uncle Ronnie?'

I give Ben a sip of the water and Toby tells him everything that's happened.

'OK, Spence, give us a hand to sit up a bit.'

We try to get Ben up but he's still too dizzy.

'Look at the pillow where your head has been! It's soaked in blood!'

Poor Ben. Toby helps him to take a drink lying on his back.

'Toby, take one of those clean pillow cases off the bed you were on. I'll put it under Ben's head.'

Ben lies back onto his side and closes his eyes. For a second both Toby and I are worried, but Ben opens one eye and winks at Toby...

'It's OK you two, I'm fine, but I'm not up for anything involving moving my head until it feels better!'

I can't tell you how glad Toby and I are feeling now Ben looks as though he's on the mend. Now to rescue Dad and Uncle Steven!

'Toby, can you stay with Ben? I promise I'll get some help this time.'

'Yeah, but how are you going to get help?'

'Well, I've got an idea, I'm not going to say it out loud, but it just might work. Trust me, Toby. *I'll be back!*'

# Chapter 9

# *Goat Horn Point*

I leave my rucksack with Toby and make my way back to the camp.

I unzip my wetsuit, retrieve my compass, which is still tied around my neck, and take a bearing.

My plan is to get help for Ben first and then throw in a red herring! And that's not a fish. I expect these men are still listening to their VHF radio; well, I'm going to feed them some right prawn crackers (and by that I mean duff information)!

I arrive back at the beach. *Splash* is bobbing up and down against the wooden leg of the pier. It's nearly too shallow to climb in yet, so I jump down into the water, untie her painter from the pier and wade out.

Leaving it until the last possible minute to jump into *Splash*, I settle the oars into their rowlocks and attempt to row towards the channel. Hopefully Grandad's launch will still be stuck on the mud where I left her, wherever that is. Grandad's launch must be around here somewhere...

*Bump!*

'Hooray and hoorah! Ker-ching!'

I jump into the launch. I tie off *Splash* attaching her onto one of the brass mooring cleats.

I turn to Channel 16.

> 'Mayday, Mayday, Mayday.
> 'This is Grandad's launch, Grandad's launch.
> 'Ben urgently needs to see a doctor.
> 'He's been knocked out by a gun.
> 'Toby's OK. I'm OK.
> 'We're in the house on Monkey Island.
> 'The smugglers have gone.
> 'I'm heading back to Poole Quay with the container to give it to the police.
> 'Please send a doctor urgently for Ben.
> 'Over.'

That should do it.

They won't expect me to be sneaking up on them. Not after that message. That should be enough bait to keep them away from Monkey Island. If I'm really lucky they'll come looking for me near Poole Quay. Hopefully the police will realize there's a red herring in that message as they have already got the container.

I just wait and see if Portland Coastguard acknowledges my duff information.

> 'Mayday Grandad's launch.
> 'This is Portland Coastguard.
> 'Received Mayday.'

* * *

I switch the radio off and quickly untie the painter and jump back into *Splash*. Picking up the oars I push off back into the channel heading for Goat Horn Point!

The tide takes *Splash* off in the right direction.

The good news is as I pull away from Monkey Island I can see much further. The mist is continuing to clear. I can see the next two channel marks.

As *Splash* gently moves into deeper water she starts to drift along and I don't even have to row.

Out of the mist, to my right is a long wooden pier! This must be Goat Horn Point. The hot sunshine is burning through the black rubber of my wetsuit. Boy do I need a drink of water!

The visibility is now so good I can see the end of Brownsea Island and even the chain ferry crossing at the Haven. More importantly I can see a large white sailing boat which looks rather out of place, moored far too close to the shallows just off of Goat Horn Point. She looks as though she's aground.

'Yes!'

This must be it! A really big white boat too. There's a boarding ladder hanging over her stern I can use. But I can't see *Dougal* or the men's speedboat. I expect they're off looking for that red herring!

Grabbing onto her gunwale I put my feet onto the steel boarding ladder that goes right down into the water. Unfortunately *Splash* is making quite a racket clunking against the big boat.

79

I climb the ladder, tying *Splash* alongside. The boat is called *Big Daddy*. Standing in the cockpit, nothing looks suspicious. The main hatch is all padlocked up; it doesn't look as though any one is here at all.

It really is a posh boat; it's even got a drinks tray around the compass. Cool!

I walk softly across the deck and peer through the windows; I can't see anything because the curtains are drawn. There are a further two hatches and what looks like a sail locker on the foredeck. A quick search reveals nothing.

I need to look inside the boat but I can't just break in.

*And then all of a sudden I hear something!*

I shout. I shout my one-eyed head off!

'Dad, Dad, Uncle Steven, is that you? It's Spencer!'

Suddenly I feel the boat rocking. I hear some banging against one of the bulkheads and the sound of loud moaning.

I pull at the padlock, but it's useless. I'll have to find something to break the padlock off!

Turning round I pull open all the lockers in the cockpit and settle for the biggest weapon of my choice. Yes a ruddy big winch handle. That should make an impact! I take several swings at the padlock … and then Bingo! With one powerful swing the lock is well and truly busted.

'Dad, where are you? It's Spencer.'

I crash through the cabin door and enter. What I see takes my breath away…

## Chapter 10

# Murder on Monkey Island

'Dad! Dad!'

Dad and Uncle Steven are all tied up with rope and tape all around their mouths. Now that *is* going to hurt.

I untie them both as quickly as I can. Dad is in tears, but he should be happy because I've rescued him; he reaches out and squeezes my shoulder, luckily my left one (not my splattered right one).

'Spencer, I think your Dad has broken his ankle. The short man pushed him through the hatchway and he fell badly.'

'I'm OK, son, I'm OK... Oh, Spencer...'

And he holds me so close that I burst out crying. Some superhero I am!

'Dad and Uncle Steven, I think we should get out of here before those men come back.'

'OK, Spencer. What's happened to Toby and Ben?'

'They're both on Monkey Island and Ben's hurt. He got walloped on the head, but he should be OK. I've already called for a doctor. I really think we should get off of this boat and go back to Monkey Island. The men have got *Dougal* and their speedboat and they can easily catch up with us.

Uncle Steven and I help Dad up. We make our way out of the boat.

'Dad, I'll just be a minute. I'm going to send a message to Abbey, the police inspector who's helping us.'

Back into the main saloon, above the chart table is their VHF radio. Switching a few buttons I manage to get to Channel 16.

'Mayday. Mayday.

'Spencer has rescued his Dad and Uncle Steven.

'Going back to Monkey Island.

'Dad has got a broken ankle.

'The Smugglers' boat is called *Big Daddy*. It's moored off Goat Horn Point.

'Over.'

Then I have another idea. Up on the wall, next to a red fire extinguisher, is an EPIRB (Emergency Position Indicating Radio Beacon). I pull off the plastic cable and turn it on. Ha! Now that will silently transmit this boat's exact position. How cool am I (as Jimmy would say).

*Something on the chart table catches my eye... It's a photograph or picture of a snake. It's drawn, it doesn't look real. Up closer I can see it's drawn on someone's skin; it's a tattoo. There's something weird but familiar about it which makes me feel cold and uncomfortable...*

Anyway, back out to Dad, who is settling himself down into *Splash*.

'What did you do, Spencer?'

'I sent a message to the police using the VHF radio. Oh yes, I also accidentally on purpose set off their EPIRB.'

Dad and Uncle Steven nod their heads in approval.

Uncle Steven and Dad ask me all sorts of questions about Ben and Toby and how I managed to navigate and contact the police.

'Well, Spencer, I think you deserve a medal. You really are a very brave and strong lad. And putting two and two together, you're the one who damaged their speedboat?'

'Yes, but it made them very angry.'

Dad gently hugs me. I'm really glad Uncle Steven is rowing; my shoulder is not feeling that good!

Uncle Steven continues to head further over to the right of the channel.

'I'm taking her closer in, I think we must be quite near our landing place. This time let's keep *Splash* hidden – we'll pull her up onto the beach and hide her. I think between us with our various injuries we can just about manage that.'

'What shall we do then, Steve?'

'I'm going up to the house; I must see my boys.'

'I'm going to have to stay pretty much where we land because of this busted ankle.'

Poor Dad, his ankle is very swollen and purple. I know it must really hurt. It makes me feel sick looking at it. My dad looks so very grey and tired.

\* \* \*

*Splash* grinds over the shallows. We haul her up the beach and hide her in the bushes.

'Ronnie, I'm off to get Ben and Toby. Stay here, I'll be back soon. Spence, do you know where Grandad's launch is?'

'Close, I think, but just ever so slightly stuck in the mud. I did throw the anchor over.'

Uncle Steven pats me on my shoulder. Of course I wish he hadn't!

'Good luck, Steve.'

Dad and I move onto the beach. He drops to the ground. I slip my life-jacket off and place it under his head.

'Thanks, Spencer. What will your mum have to say when she finds out what's been happening?'

'She already knows.'

'How?' Dad seems a bit worried by this piece of information.

'Well, after I made the Mayday call, somehow they traced Mum and Jimmy and they were on their way to Poole Quay. I suppose they must know everything.'

'Well, that will save me trying to explain it all!'

'Hey, Dad, look over there!'

Pointing over to the channel, just through the trees I can just see Grandad's launch.

'I've got the key in my jacket pocket, Spencer.'

'Why don't I wade out to the launch and call up Portland Coastguard? They can tell me what's happened to Ben and Toby. I can tell them where we are and that you've broken your ankle.'

'No, Uncle Steven told us to wait here.'

'Well, *you* can wait here and I'll go, but I'll be back soon and you can see me all the time if you sit up a bit.'

'OK, but put your life-jacket back on and come straight back.'

'Yes, Dad.'

Wading out into the cool water is refreshing and with Dad so close I begin to feel safe.

Climbing back into the launch is a bit of a problem. It looks all too easy from the outside, but without a boarding ladder it is really difficult. I manage to bounce high enough to pivot my stomach on the gunwale then slither over onto the deck, rather like a sea lion sliding into the water.

'Portland Coastguard. Portland Coastguard.
'This is Grandad's launch.
'Back on Monkey Island.
'Dad's ankle still broken, purple and green.
'Are Ben and Toby OK?
'Can someone please help my Dad?'

I look back out to the shoreline. I see Dad hobble out into the open with his hands up. What's he doing? Instinctively I hit the deck!

What's going on? I force myself to snatch a glance above the gunwale, just enough time to take in the whole scene. Dad and Uncle Steven are on the beach with the *pirates* behind them. *And the pirates are aiming their guns at them.*

I hold my breath. Then someone shouts.

*'OK, Captain Birdseye, we know you're there. Get over here or I'll shoot your dad.'*

Oh crud!

# Chapter 11

# *Revenge*

I have to go. *I have to go.* I lift up my head just above the gunwale. As I do I pick up the handset and make one more transmission, turning away to disguise my actions.

'Mayday.
'It's Spencer Drew.
'Got caught by the pirates.
'They've got guns.
'Will lead them into trap.
'Please be there!
'PS. Up shit-creek!'

End of transmission. Turning back I let the handset drop to the floor. Facing the beach, my audience awaits. I slip back into the water.

Although I am scared out of my mind, somewhere deep inside of me a tiger's strength and courage is rising...

And these words keep popping into my head.

*There is ALWAYS a consequence to bad behaviour.*

* * *

As a little boy I knew this all too well. Similarly, good behaviour had rewards but these two men had not yet learnt this. Well it was about time they did!

I emerge from the water with the patch covering my tiger's eye. Now it's pirates versus pirates!

I can see the fear on my Dad's face as I approach the smugglers. He turns to one of the pirates...

'He's just a boy...'

And then the man kicks Dad in his bad ankle. Falling to his knees, Dad howls out in agony. 'Dad!' I shout out. They really shouldn't have done that!

Uncle Steven leans forward and looks as though he might attack both men, but before another step is taken a loud deafening gunshot is fired. Uncle Steven drops to the ground clutching his leg. I can see the blood, trickling down his leg and onto the sand.

They have shot Uncle Steven!

'*You should have listened to us, Captain Birdseye, look what you've made us do. Now give us back what you took from us and nobody will get killed.*'

'I don't have it here, I buried it somewhere else.'

'*Show us.*'

Pointing their guns for me to move off and show them. I don't move. I'm staring at my Dad and Uncle Steven. Dad has taken his shirt off and is wrapping it around Uncle Steven's leg.

One of the pirates screams at me. '*Move it! Or*

*the next bullet will go through his head!'* He is pointing the gun at Dad's head.

As I walk away from the beach, I can hear Dad crying.
'I love you, Dad.' I shout.

Walking along to our camp I undo my wetsuit zip only to be spun round and find a gun up my left nostril!
'*What you up to?'*
'Compass. I need to follow a compass bearing to locate the exact position I buried your container.'
'*I don't trust you with your stupid pirate's patch on, Cyclops. Take it off.'*
'*No!'*
'*Nobody says no to me.'*
'I can't take it off. I'm part of a top secret experiment. I have a hyper-biotechnical tiger's eye that is used for transmitting top secret information to the government through my highly developed laser transmitter.'

The pirates start to laugh.
'*Come on, let's go, just take us to our stuff, he knows the score if he's lying.'* And he cocks his gun.
Unless my last message to Portland Coastguard was intercepted, I feel for sure we're all doomed.

We walk back towards the lookout tree. I try and buy the police some time and take quite a long way round the island until the pirates begin to get edgy and scare me with their threats.

'Do you think we're stupid? I know we've passed that tree at least twice in the past fifteen minutes. This isn't a game, kid. I've got four bullets left.'

'I've just remembered I forgot to bring the shovel!'

'Yeah, well you'll just have to use your hands.'

Good, I do hope so. Of course I'm dead meat if the police aren't there, so who cares!

I guess it's now or never.

Arriving close to the Monkey Island latrine, I can't see anything which suggests help has arrived.

I stop walking.

'Is this the place?'

'Over there, in front of that bush.'

The two men are over there like a flash. They are down on their knees and clearing away the sticks and leaves. They are facing me whilst they dig.

Something beyond them in the trees starts to move.

*Oh my God!* I'm suddenly aware that surrounding us are what seem like hundreds of camouflaged soldiers!

My heart is racing.

I must keep the pirates facing forwards towards me.

I know the one thing that will get their attention.

'Hey, you two, look at this.'

I lift up my pirate's patch and as I open my eyelid a blinding light once again erupts from my tiger's eye, piercing the shadows of the trees.

The pirates are like rabbits caught in headlights; their mouths are wide open, but nothing comes out.

And as they cover their eyes with their hands to shield themselves from the shards of white light, they start to smell what is on their fingers.

'What is this?'

'I think my hands are covered in shit!'

I think they've reached the cesspit! They stand up and smell their brown hands. It won't take them long to work out the soil analysis.

Exit stage left I think... Patch down, run like crazy!

*Go Spencer Go.*

Yes, run! Off I go, just like the tiger in my dream, I seem to be taking huge leaps over things, faster than I've ever known. Running for my life...

*Bang!*

I can't feel any pain. Missed me.

There is another loud gunshot from way behind me, which brings my chase to an end. I can hear a lot of shouting then silence. I stand still for a moment, clutching a tree for cover, catching my breath.

'We meet again Spencer Drew!'

'Hey! That made me jump. Who are you?'

* * *

A tall soldier with curly dark hair and dark skin seems to have appeared from nowhere.

'Well done, young man. You have to come with me now to a place of safety.'

'But what about Dad and Uncle Steven?'

'*Spencer, Spencer Drew.*' Someone is hailing me on a megaphone.

'I'd better go, sir; I want to see what happened to those pirates. I'll see you later.'

'Yes, we will meet again. You have something that belongs to me.'

'Oh, you can have the compass now.'

Slipping off the compass I thrust it into the soldier's hand... The tip of a tail...

'Bye, and thanks.'

As I move away from the soldier, turning back into the shadow of the trees, a shaft of sunlight glints on the edge of the compass in the soldier's hand, but something else registers... His hand! It's the photograph. I mean, the tattoo pattern of a snake! From the tip of a tail to a hissing, spitting face.

Unsure of what to do, I make a mad run in the opposite direction, only to be greeted by nearly a whole platoon of camouflaged soldiers. I turn back, expecting the soldier to still be with me, but he has already disappeared back into the shadows.

The soldiers start to clap as I get closer. Clapping and whistling. I look over my shoulder just to check someone famous like Jonathan Ross or Kylie Minogue hasn't just arrived and upstaged me; I conclude the applause is directed at me. It's about sodding time!

* * *

Deep into the sea of soldiers, deep into the cheering and clapping, lie the two evil men, this time with *their* hands and feet tied. As I approach them the horrors of their cruelty to Ben, Dad and Uncle Steven flash through my mind.

I bend down on one knee and they raise their heads to face me.

'Remember this, and remember it well! *There is always a consequence to bad behaviour!'*

Keeping my eyes focused on their mean ugly faces, I lift up my patch.

And from under the darkness of the trees the fierce explosion of brilliant light blasts in to the faces of these evil men, making them cry out in pain as they are blinded by the intense luminosity.

'Aaahh!'

'Look and remember. I have the eye of a tiger!'

Well, that serves them right! I put back my cheap plastic pirate's patch. Even the soldiers can't believe what they have just seen. What a great party trick!

Fast approaching is a group of figures. They look like the St John's Ambulance Brigade band, but why would they come here?

No, it's the police. There's a lady, I wonder if that's Abbey.

'Well done, Spencer, you are a hero!'

'Thank you, but can someone go and help my Dad and Uncle Steven, and can anyone tell me how Ben is?'

'They are all going to be fine. They are already being cared for in Poole Hospital.'

'Please can you take me to see them?'

'Certainly, Spencer. You know you would make an excellent policeman.'

'Well, I hope you don't mind, but I had rather thought I'd be the next James Bond!'

And then all around me the soldiers start to laugh and clap and begin humming the theme tune to James Bond. I guess that did sound a bit big-headed!

## Chapter 12

# Back to The Quay

On the way back to Poole Quay, I ride in a really fast police launch. I think the skipper broke the 10-knot speed limit in the harbour! But I didn't say anything. I didn't want to get him into trouble.

We moor up alongside the Fish Shamble Steps.

'Excuse me, Abbey, I've been meaning to ask you, what was in that container I took from those men?'

'Diamonds. Lots of very valuable diamonds.'

'How much are they worth?'

'I don't know exactly, but more than a million pounds!'

'Wow! I forgot to ask one more thing, did you catch the boss? And the other boat with the broken engine?'

'Not yet, but we're working on it. Oh yes, and the owner of these diamonds would like to thank you personally. When you are quite recovered you have been invited to collect a reward from the owner's head office in London.'

'Cool-a-rama!'

Stepping off of the police launch with Abbey, I

can see Mum and Jimmy coming over towards me. I run, Mum and Jimmy run, I'm so happy to feel this safe again with Mum's arms around me. My strength is draining out of me and I suddenly feel weak.

The tiger's eye that had given me so much strength seems to have weakened and my good eye is letting me down badly, weeping over my Mum's lovely warm coat. Too ashamed to show her my tear-stained face, I hold her tightly in our group hug that lasts forever and ever.

Then I remember. Pulling abruptly away, I blurt out, 'Mum, Dad's hurt, I have to go and see him. Ben and Uncle Steven too.'

'I know, sweetheart. Come on, they've provided a police car to take us to Poole Hospital. One of the doctors will need to take a look at you too when we get there.'

'Oh, I'm OK! My shoulder's a bit wonky-flaky.'

'I think they may have to give you an emergency *bath* at the very least, Spencer!' says Jimmy.

'Yes, I do whiff a bit. But I bet I smell a lot sweeter than those two pirates do after what they dug up!'

Mum and Jimmy don't know what I mean, but I can't wait to tell Ben and Toby. Now that will make them laugh!

I spent the rest of the day and a whole night in Poole Hospital. I didn't mind because Dad, Ben and Uncle Steven were there too.

It's really weird, but trouble seems to follow me everywhere. When they X-rayed my shoulder the machine blew up! Can you believe it? Anyway, they strapped my shoulder up which feels so much better and gave me something to take away the pain. I'm going to have an X-ray in Bournemouth hospital tomorrow to make sure nothing's broken.

It's funny; after I fell asleep a doctor came in to speak to me. The weirdest thing is he looked exactly like that tall soldier on Monkey Island. It didn't seem real. Maybe it was a dream. I wanted to ask him about his tattoo, but something stopped me. I can remember bits of the conversation.

'We meet again, Spencer Drew.'

'Aren't you the soldier on Monkey Island?'

'I am many things, Spencer Drew. Now calm yourself and answer these questions.'

He asked me some strange questions about my horrific accident when I lost my eye. Could I remember this? Could I remember that? And he *really* wanted to know where my lucky stone was. Of course I lied and told him I'd lost the stone on Monkey Island. The man was *very* angry about this and stormed out of the room. How weird was that? And he didn't even ask me anything about the diamond thieves.

After he left my room, I pulled out my lucky stone which was still tied around my neck.

Anyway, the good news is Dad, Uncle Steven and Ben all recovered from their injuries. Mum let me stay in Poole for most of the summer holidays so I could help Dad get better. We even got to go out on *Splash*, after Dad's plaster came off. Uncle Steven has still got scaffolding attached to his leg. So he has to be driven everywhere. Ben says he would drive his Dad about if he was seventeen. Uncle Steven says he's glad Ben is only fifteen!

Mum stayed in Poole for a while, too. We spent a lot of time helping Chief Inspector Abbey Brook, answering lots of questions about what happened.

The police were very interested in the soldier who approached me on Monkey Island. On the other hand, when I told them he'd turned up in my hospital bedroom as a doctor, the police said I'd had a flashback. I'm not so sure...

The police never caught the Boss or Metal Mickey (whoever he was); and *Big Daddy* was found, run aground just off Goat Horn Point. Eventually we found out it belonged to a man from St Peters Port in Guernsey, which is one of the Channel Islands. He had it stolen nearly six months earlier. I expect he was really pleased to get it back.

Abbey had all of our boats and camping equipment returned safely.

I suppose I will never forget my summer holiday in Poole. I wanted an adventure, but maybe not one that scary! At least I got to see Ben and Toby loads.

Since that moment on Monkey Island when Toby accidentally gained a glimpse of my tiger's eye, he has never asked me to reveal it again.

I'm back in London now. Jimmy will be home from work soon and he promised me we could throw the rugby ball to each other outside in the courtyard for a while before dinner.

I'll be starting my new school in September called Night Wights, apparently it's a school for children with special abilities – I wonder what kind of adventures I'll have there? It's funny, but that scares me even more than facing evil diamond-smuggling pirates. Jimmy says it's normal to be a bit nervous before beginning a new school.

Perhaps it's not important, but I had the dream again last night of the tiger. I don't know why, but it feels as if the dream is trying to tell me something important. Maybe I'll work it out later...

Oh, and I've got an appointment with Q next week. Wait till I tell him how cool the eye's been.

And if you're wondering where my lucky stone is now, well I won't tell you, only Dad and I know. Something tells me there's more to this lucky stone than meets the eye (ha ha).

The End

Spencer Drew will return in the sequel to
*Adventure on Monkey Island*: the epic
*Eye Of The Tiger*

# Spencer Drew's Glossary of Nautical Jargon

**aft**        towards stern of ship
**bow**        front pointy end of ship
**bulkhead**   partition in interior of ship
**cleat**      a piece of wood or iron with two projecting ends round which ropes are secured
**gunwales**   upper edge of ship's side
**helming**    steering/driving
**lubbers**    unskilled seamen
**painter**    line at bow of boat for tying it up
**pontoon**    floating wooden bridge or walkway
**port** .     left
**reciprocal** move backwards and forwards
**rowlocks**   appliance on gunwale of boat serving as point of leverage for oar
**rudder**     flat piece hinged to boat's stern for steering
**starboard**  right
**stern**      rear part or back end of ship
**tacking**    taking a boat on a zigzag course

**throttle**   device controlling the amount of fuel entering a boat's engine and thereby its speed

**tiller**   lever to move the rudder and steer the boat

Can't wait for the sequel, *Eye of The Tiger*?

Here's a taster...

It's my appointment today with Q, my brilliant eye surgeon. Mum is real edgy, 'cos she thinks I'm going crackers. I know something weird is happening to me, well only in my head – everything else seems to be in good working order.

My dreams seem so real and there's this guy... I mean that stranger I met on Monkey Island and again in Poole hospital. The one no one believes exists; well he just keeps popping into my head day and night. He always asks me questions about my lucky stone. I mean what's that all about? I have to lie to him obviously so he doesn't find out where I've hidden it, 'cos only Dad and I know that.

'Good morning, Spencer and Mary, nice to see you both again.' 'Hi Q, I mean Dr Quinn.'

'Please come through... Would you mind taking your eye patch off Spencer? I'd like to examine your prosthesis.'

'Excuse me Dr Quinn, may I have a word with you in private?'

Oh no...

'Mum! I'm OK.'

'Please, son, I just need to have a grown up chat with the doctor. It'll be OK. I promise.'

'No strait jackets, Mum; they are *so* yesterday's fashion!'

'Yes, of course, Mary, we'll just pop through into my secretary's office. Don't look so worried, Spencer. It can't be that bad.'

Thanks, Mum! Watching Mum and Q close the door behind them, I slip off my pirate's patch and sit on Q's state of the art swivel chair behind his large desk. The desire to find a game to play on his computer is running very high. Instead I'll spin round in his swivel chair. Fun but nauseating, I'd better stop that...

Come on, Mum, make it snappy, I don't want to be stuck in here all day. I can hear the muffled voice of Q through the wall. Dragging the chair further back I put my feet up on Q's desk, opening my left eye lid, allowing the brilliant laser beam light to erupt from my Hyper-biotechnical Tiger's eye. I begin to stare hard at the wall, craning my ears to try and overhear Mum and Q's conversation.

What's that smell? Horse manure! Don't tell me I've put my foot in something unsavoury!

'WHAT!'

Something is distorting the surface of the wall at the exact same place I am staring! Bloody hell! The wall has dissolved; I mean I can see through it into the next room. Dropping my feet to the ground and sliding closer to Q's desk, I move my laser beam light from my tiger's eye across the wall and as I do it opens a sort of round portal about a foot wide in diameter then closes as I move past revealing the next bit I am focused on.

But how am I doing this, which eye is it I am

seeing with? There's Q... He hasn't even noticed what I've just done to the wall. Does that mean he can't see it? What's he saying? I concentrate harder and try to lip read. Q is coming through loud and clear.

'I think it's time I told you the truth about what really happened to your son.'